by Kel McDonald & Jose Pimienta

strange and amazing

inquiry@ironcircus.com www.ironcircus.com

Words | Colors
Kel McDonald

Line Art
Jose Pimienta

Publisher
C. Spike Trotman

Editor
Andrea Purcell

Art Director | Cover Design
Matt Sheridan

Print Technician | Book Design
Beth Scorzato

Proofreader
Abby Lehrke

Published by
Iron Circus Comics
329 West 18th Street, Suite 604
Chicago, IL 60616

First Edition October 2021

ISBN 978-1-945820-89-2

Printed in China

STARS, HIDE YOUR FIRE

Publisher's Cataloging-In-Publication Data
(Prepared by The Donohue Group, Inc.)

Names: McDonald, Kel, author, colorist. | Pimienta, Jose, illustrator. | Spike, 1978- publisher. | Purcell, Andrea, editor. | Sheridan, Matt, 1978- designer. | Scorzato, Beth, designer.
Title: Stars, hide your fire / by Kel McDonald [words & colors] & Jose Pimienta [line art] ; [publisher, C. Spike Trotman ; editor, Andrea Purcell ; art director, cover design, Matt Sheridan ; print technician, book design, Beth Scorzato ; proofreader, Abby Lehrke].
Description: First edition. | Chicago, IL : Iron Circus Comics, 2021. | Interest age level: 008-012. | Summary: "Two modern-day teens in a dead-end small town and their 100-year-old new friend face off against a supernatural trickster with nefarious intentions who has promised them eternal life"–Provided by publisher.
Identifiers: ISBN 9781945820892
Subjects: LCSH: Teenagers–Comic books, strips, etc. | Tricksters–Comic books, strips, etc. | Future life–Comic books, strips, etc. | CYAC: Teenagers–Fiction. | Tricksters–Fiction. | Future life–Fiction. | LCGFT: Paranormal comics. | Graphic novels.
Classification: LCC PZ7.7.M438 St 2021 | DDC 741.5973 [Fic]–dc23

For in my way it lies. Stars, hide your fires;
Let not light see my black and deep desires.

Macbeth
Act 1, Scene 4

Hurry up, Darra!
I thought I heard something.
You're being paranoid.

I just don't want to get caught.
Fine then.

Stay here.

HEY! Wait up!

Andrea!
If you are so worried about getting caught, you should stop shouting.

Just... I don't know...
Be careful.

And how on earth do we get in?
There's a little crack.

Maybe we can find something to pry it open a little. At least enough for us to get in.

Do you really think we'll find a ghost?
No. Probably not.

It would be wicked cool if we did though.
Yeah, it would!

That's how I know it won't happen.

'cause nothing cool happens here.

I can't find anything to pry the door.

Maybe if I smash a window we can climb in.
WAIT! DON'T!

We could get in a lot of trouble for that. More than if it's just trespassing.

And the door might be old enough that we can force it open.

sigh Fine.

ERRRR!

The rock might be easier.
Errr. And this is safer.
I don't know about safer. Looks like a good chance of tetanus.

Could you help push? Maybe?

EEEEEEEEKK

Great. Let's go.

Aw man. I think I ruined my shirt.
Whoa.

This place is amazingly creepy.

When was the last time you think someone was here? Probably like 100 years.
More like 60.

In history class they said it was open from 1850 to 1955.

Or maybe it was 1957.

Neat. Do you remember what happened?

Um, I think the company got bought and moved to Switzerland.
Makes sense.

Why stay here when you could be anywhere?

I donno. Switzerland's kinda cold. Brr.

No thank you.
Hahaha. I would take cold over bored.

So where do you think the ghost might be?

There's not gonna be a ghost.

CLANK

Wh-what was that?

I donno but I'm gonna find out.

What!? No. It could be the cops!

Why would cops be IN here?

Okay, but we should still leave. It could be like a junkie squatting in here or a coyote or... something else dangerous.

I just wanna look. Then we'll leave.

W-w-well I'm leaving.

Just give me a minute...

Darra! Check this out!

sigh

Ow.
You okay?

My butt might be sore for a day, but I'll live.

You won't believe this but...

I saw the ghost!

Are you sure it wasn't a person? I'm pretty sure I saw someone.

You're being paranoid. I got pictures.

Fatima's Mart
THE·BEE·TOY
WAL WAT
SALE

Ugh! I'm such an idiot.
GIFTS
DINING

I left the flash on.

The other pictures came out good though.
I guess.

Maybe I was just seeing things. It was too cool to be true.
WAL WAT

AH!

Watch where you're going, Steve!

You owe me an apology!

Let me get that for you, Mr. O'Neil.

There you are!

You're supposed to be stocking shelves.

There. Have a nice day.

*sigh*Come on. Back to work.

Hey!

Are you two waiting for your parents to pick you up or something?
Mart
No.

Well, there's no loitering. So you gotta get out of here.

And go where?
Somewhere. Just find a way to entertain yourselves.

Come on, Andrea.

Maybe the ghost is real and that's who Steve is talking to all the time.
Wal-Lex

Hmp. That'd be a nicer story than just too many concussions from football.

My mom said it was binge drinking pickled his brain.
Maybe your mom's right. Either way he's pretty much stuck here.
Wal-Lex

Maybe. Or she is just using it as a scare tactic.

Don't drink or do drugs. 'Else you'll end up with no future.
HA HA HA

That's really good. You sound just like her.
She's so concerned about the future that... hmm...

You okay?
I guess.

We just had a fight this morning.

I overslept and missed a pre SAT class she signed me up for.

90's Roller Ring
I thought that was for sophomores?
THAT'S WHAT I SAID!

We just started high school. I'm not ready to think about college. But she says I need to go to a make-up class this afternoon.

Well, just tell her what she wants to hear. Then skip it.

That will just get us in another fight.

Come on. We can go back to the factory and try to find out what I saw.

I think we should go AFTER I have class.
90's
ller Ring

Fine.
90's
Roller Rin
90's
Roller Rin

Casita
PHARMACY

It's not that I don't want to go. I just don't want to get in more trouble with my mom.
I said it's fine.

I should probably get going.

I'll see ya later.

UFF!

sigh

CLKS!!

Hello?

Is someone there?

h-help me

Oh, it's you. The girl from last night.

Wait, what?
Who are you?

Call me Carmen. You were here last night, weren't you?

How-how'd you know that?

You tried to take my picture.

What do you mean your picture? Were you messing with my friend and I last night?

And how'd you know we-

HOLY CRAP!

Are you okay?
This place is weakening me.

Weakening you?

Andrea.
GAH!

There's too much iron here. It's weakening my magic.

My hero.

What are you?

I mean you're not a ghost. Are you a witch or something?

I'm a member of the fair folke. All this iron...

I couldn't get out. All the doors are made of the stuff and I can't touch it.

Oh. Hold on then.
Oh cool.
How'd you get in there if you can't touch the doors?
I was trapped there by an awful mortal.
There is this man who I granted a wish for and now he's gotten what he wanted he's trying to get rid of me. He trapped me in there so I couldn't stop him.
A wish?
Yes. I can only stay here if I have a deal with a mortal

Here? Why would you wanna stay here?

OH WHY WOULDN'T I?!
You have cars and skyscrapers and curry and clubs that are open all night and theater and...

Music!

Oh, by here you... don't mean... in town.

Even the sun feels nicer.

Where would you be if you weren't here?

A bad place.

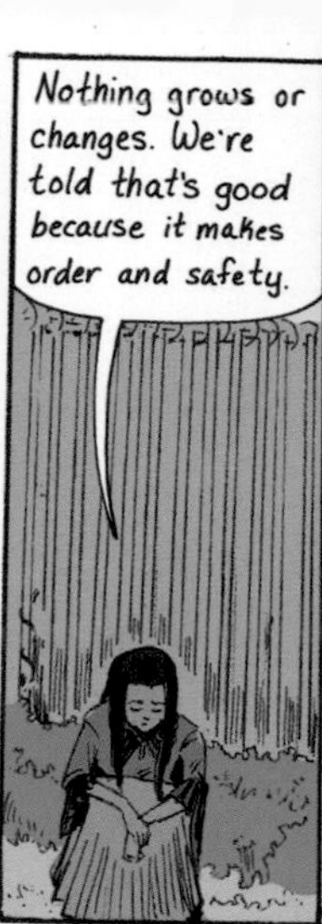
Nothing grows or changes. We're told that's good because it makes order and safety.

But everything is dull and the same, day after day.

We have to make do with pale copies of what you mortals are doing. Which just makes it worse.

Because we know about all the amazing things out of reach.

Not that a mortal would understand.

I do though.

You do?

Yeah. Is there a way to let you stay here without being attached to someone else?

I would need someone else to find my fairy ring and make a deal with me.

That will be hard. Most mortals don't believe in magic anymore.

What would you give a mortal in a deal with you?

OH! EVERYTHING! ANYTHING!
Adventure! Excitement!
I could show them the whole world.

But they'd need to find my fairy ring.

I could try looking for it. Then you could lead the person you make a deal with there.

Whoever they are.

You would do that? That would be wonderful!

It's okay. There isn't much else to do around here.

Where should I start? And what's it look like?

It's a ring of dead grass. It WAS in the woods.

But that was 100 years ago. It might not be woods anymore.

5:40
Andrea
Just got out of PreSAT class. What are you up to?
Wanna check the factory again?
You there now?
Did you go w/o me?
Where Are you?
Your Mom says you're not home.

You better be here.

Um... hello?
GAH!

You scared me.
Sorry... I...

What are you doing?
What's it look like? I'm cleaning these up.

Oh.

Aren't flowers and leaves drying good for the grass growing or something?

Yes. But this one is foxglove and this other one is deadly nightshade.

If we leave them out, animals might eat them and get sick.

But it's okay if we just touch them?
Just make sure you don't have any cuts.

My name's Darra.

Liam.

These are really pretty.
Most poisonous things are.

This will sound weird but...

Were you here last night?

Because my friend Andrea and I snuck in here last night to look for this ghost and I think I saw you or someone who looks like you.

Did you see the ghost? You have to stay away! She's dangerous!

What? The ghost is real?!

Her name's Carmen and she's not a ghost;

She's a demon.

Well, maybe the ghost is something else or just a story. But Carmen was here last night.

These come from her magic.

Liam, it's not nice to make fun of people.
What?

Just because my friend and I were ghost hunting doesn't mean I'll believe anything.

Oh.

You're right. I shouldn't have said anything.

BZZ
BZZ

BUZZBUZZ

5:55
Andrea
Sorry. My battery died. XP
but, oh man, you won't believe this.
I found the ghost!!! (O_O)
Except she's not a ghost. Her name is Carmen and she is magic.
It's wicked awesome we gotta meet tmrw.

Um,... what'd you say the demon's name was again?
Carmen.

What's she look like? How do you know she is a demon?

You won't believe me.
I'll try.

No, you won't.

Please.

If she's really dangerous, I think my friend might be in trouble.

I know she's a demon because I accidentlly made a deal with her 100 years ago.

What?

I was gonna run away from home and came across a fairy ring in the woods. At least I thought it was a fairyring.
A fairy ring?
THANK YO
THANK YO
THANK YO
Um, it's a circle of mushrooms, flowers, or grass that's growing quicker. Fairies dance there so you can catch or summon them there.
Well, my mom told me about them. So I tried to catch one.
Because I... *sigh* well, I don't even know anymore.
And around midnight she appeared in a swirl of these flowers.
But you just said she was a demon.
I didn't know at first.

She offered to let me stay young, so I wouldn't have to grow up.
She somehow knew that's why I wanted to run away.
It was fine at first. But then I found out she was hurting people to keep me young.
I tried to stop her with iron. It did nothing. She can't be a fairy. She has to be a demon.
If you're 100, wouldn't you already be a grown up to people back then?

In some ways. I worked here with my dad and a few of my brothers.
It was hard. But anywhere I went I'd probably have to work in a place like this. At least my family was near here.
But then two of my older brothers fought in the Great War.
One died.
The other came back with half his face.
I guess I'm a coward.
No.
I actually feel silly for being scared of my future, of the SATs, college, and moving away by comparison.
US

The future is always scary.

But what I did was stupid and is getting other people hurt. So I need to stop Carmen.

I don't completely believe you but I don't want my friend to get hurt. What do you got to do?

I need to find her fairy circle again and banish her.
Where is it?

The woods or what was the woods. Things have changed a bit around here.

The Great War is World War 1, right?
Um, yeah. Sorry. Should have just called it that. Like I said, things change.

WALTHAM HIGH SCHOOL

Oh man, this is so freaking cool!

WALTHAM
FOREVER
EXIT
I still don't know if I believe either of them. Maybe they overheard us last night and this is a prank.

But she FLEW, Darra!
ENTER

What are you looking at?
You, ya weirdo.
FOOD

yes!!

Mind your own business.

Mayflower
I swear she honest to god flew.

Well, there isn't a whole lot of places that are woods left.

Well, there is near the old watch factory, there's the park with the water tower, and then near the closed hospital.
JOANNES EST NOMEN EJUS

Do you know how old the hospital is? Is it 100 years old?
FOREVER

Probably. It looks kinda old timey.

I'll ask Carmen if she remembers either area.

Um... How? Did she give you a phone number or something?

Eerrr...
May flower

No... I guess not.
Health CON

She'll show up again. If this is a prank, she'll want to push it farther.

And if she's telling the truth then she needs you.

I guess.

Those poor girls.

And in their dorm room...

College is supposed to be exciting and time to grow, not get shot by some misogynist with a gun.

Did you finish your homework?
Yes.

Good. I'll finish up on the phone and then we can go over Pre SAT prep.

Can't I take a night off?
Not until the practice test results come in

If you did well, then we'll talk about a night off.

Hey, Jeanie, I'll call you back.

Sweetie, I know it's hard.

You just need to be prepared for the world after high school.

You're almost an adult.

Okay.

I'm gonna eat dinner outside.

It's nice out.
Come in if it gets too cold.

Hi, Jeanie, sorry about that.

I was just talking to Darra about her school work.
I know!

I'm so proud of her.

S.F.
B.T.
PUSSY RIOT
Silvelake
LOVE IS LOVE

Bikini Kill
SVERIGE
SKAREN
ASK ME ABOUT MY FEMINIST AGENDA
RUIDO ROSA
Myanmar
THELMA & LOUISE
HACK
Cistem
VIVE
LATNX
Hawaii
MARU TE
PROJECT TRANS KIDS
Butler
UNDOING

New York &
San Juan &
Prague &
Glendale
BOSTON MARCH
CITY HALL 9-AM
RBG
ALL
AMSTER
kidam
Andrea? Andrea, wake up.

hhmmm--
Wha...

Shhh.
It's me.

Carmen!
Shhh.

Right, sorry.

I knew this wasn't fake.

Fake?

Oh, my friend thought your story might be pulling a prank.

But I told her you were flying and that'd be pretty hard to fake.

I would really appreciate it...

If you didn't tell people about me.
THE FUTURE IS

But... I tell her everything...

Everything? Really?

So you told Darra about how I need a new human...
THE FUT

Partner.

Um,...no. I didn't tell her that.
THE FUTURE

RBG
But I told her about the fairy ring. She's smart and knows about history and stuff.

She helped me think of places from 100 years ago that still have lots of woods near them.

Well, that's okay. I guess.

THE FUTURE
So...um... your fairy circle, do you know if it was near that old factory, or a hill or a large brick building?

RBG
I definitely remember a large brick building on the edge on of the woods.
AMSTERDAM

Does that help?

Uh, yeah.

WONDERFUL!

Whoa!

Oh cool!
ABG

I'm so glad. There's nothing worse than being trapped in a dull lifeless place.

Tell me about it
NYC
RESIST

Have you traveled much over the years?
RBG

Here and there. I can't go too far from the human I'm bonded to. It was all places he picked.
GALILEO

Him sticking around here is how I figured out he was planning to toss me aside.

But if you could pick where would you go?

Hmm...

Silverlake
Los Angeles...

¡51 PRESENTE!
Caribe
Puerto Rico...

Maybe London.

That'd be wicked awesome.
THE FUTURE IS

Especially if I could shared it with someone who wants me around.
THE FUTURE

THE FUTURE

Uh, Carmen...

You're a fairy, right? I read in a book they can't lie. Is that true?

If I told you I couldn't lie, that could be a lie. You wouldn't know.

So what's the point in answering?

Reassurance.

Boston

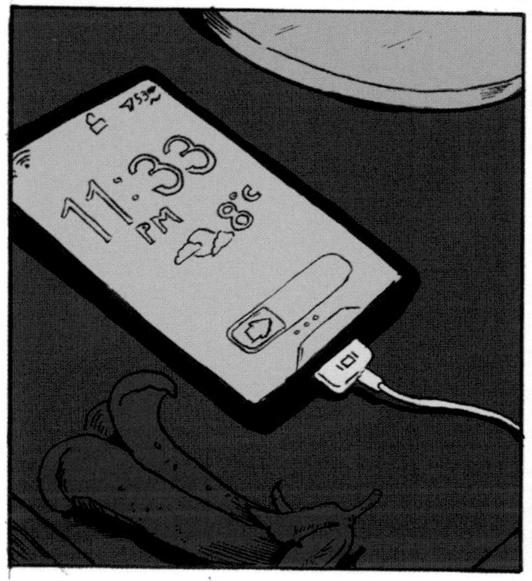
11:33
PM

It's getting a little late.

I should get going.
What?
FEMINIST
THELMA & LOUISE
RBG
BOSTON MARCH
ALL

I forget sometimes how much rest you humans need. I woke you up and that was rude.

It's okay. I don't mind.

Get some sleep. I'll be back tomorrow.

ASK ME ABOUT MY FEMINIST AGENDA
RBG

Fatimas Mart
THE BEE TOY
Wal-Lex
GIFTS
DINING
Carlos

CH-NNK
Hello?
Wal-Lex
GIFTS
DINING
Stupid wind.
JAMB
Need some help?

Where'd you come from?
Around.
Well, you shouldn't be out this late.
JAMB
Maybe you could help me with something.
Wha-
I only need a moment of your time.
Rendon's

Huh...
I'm probably just working too hard.

THANK YOU
CHELY SPRING
THE MASS POST
DESERTED OR TAKEN?
Go check:
O'Brian Farm
Sold in 1925
Whe
Jones
Farm.
noone left.
Who's there?

Heh heh.
Aren't you cold?
I'm fine.
You sure? I could help you find a warmer, drier place to sleep.
Y-yes.

I could warm you up.
I-
Stop it!
I told you I don't want this anymore!
It's what you agreed to.

I- I didn't know what would happen... What you'd do to people...
OH NO! My actions have *consequences*. How *will* I go on?
You can't get something for nothing. You wanted more time.
It has to come from somewhere.

Hmp.

You're such a child.

Going around pouting because things didn't go your way.

Are you *sure* you aren't cold?

I'm fine.
I don't want any more of your *help*.

I really need a human who's more fun.
Dammit.

Fatima's Mart
THE·BEE·TOY
Salina's

THANK
THANK
THANK

We might have bought too much.

Nah. We probably won't find this fairy ring right away.

Now we don't have to restock.

Oh, sorry. I thought I went around you.

I just gave you one.

There you are! You're supposed to be stocking shelves.
FM
PEN

I went to do that but they were already stocked.
FM

FM
STEVE

Right, right. They were stocked two days ago.

On it, sir.
FM

Hey! Are you two waiting for your parents to pick you up or something?
OPEN

This is weird.

Well, there's no loitering. So you gotta get out of here.

Are you feeling alright?

Fatima's Mart
DAN

I... I probably just didn't sleep well last night.

Thank you for asking.

Come on, let's go.

What do you think is wrong with him?

I donno. Maybe living here rotted his brain.

Mission Dragon
장난감
Hunter's

Ms.
Irene
PUSH

Carroll

Picha Pizza
Pasta Salad

CH
Chickadee Hall

That's a cute dog.

Yeah. Cute.

I bet that dog loves coming here. There probably aren't a lot of places like this near big cities.

Well, at least something enjoys it here.

Are you sure you know where you're going?

Carmen said the hospital was south of where her fairy ring was.

So I figure starting north is a good plan.
SNAP!!

You found her?

Did you get her number this time?

Uh... no. She just showed up in my room

Just showed up?

Well, she like appeared.

I told you she wasn't lying about being magic.

So you were doing homework and she just poof appeared?

No, I was sleeping. She woke me up.

You were sleeping?
Yeah.

She was just in your room while you were sleeping?

Do you know how long she was in your room? While you were sleeping?

Or why she was there?

Darra, it will be fine.

You don't *know* that.

And you don't know that it won't be fine.

ANDREA!

Andrea!

Are you okay?!

Say something.

I'm fine.

I just slipped on some leaves.

Huh.

What is it?

I donno but I'm gonna find out.

Andrea, wait!

THANK YOU
THANK YOU
THANK YOU

Uh... We probably shouldn't be here.

Uh... yeah.

What are you doing here, Darra?

You know this guy?

This um, is Liam.

The one who knows Carmen.

Liam,... do you like LIVE here?

Yes. For now at least.

But you didn't answer my question.

What are you doing here?

This is my friend Andrea.

We were looking for that fairy circle you told me about.

How'd you know to come here?

Carmen told me.

You shouldn't talk to Carmen.

Why not? Because then you can screw her over?
206

She's dangerous and can't be trusted!

And how do I know you can be trusted?

Andrea, please listen.

I know you want more than what this town can offer but...

But what?!

I'm supposed to sit quiet, go to Pre SAT classes,

and hope something interesting appears.

So I can ignore it cause I'm too scared?!

No.

But you're so eager to rush ahead that you don't see any of the red flags lining the way.
And you don't realize what you're leaving behind.

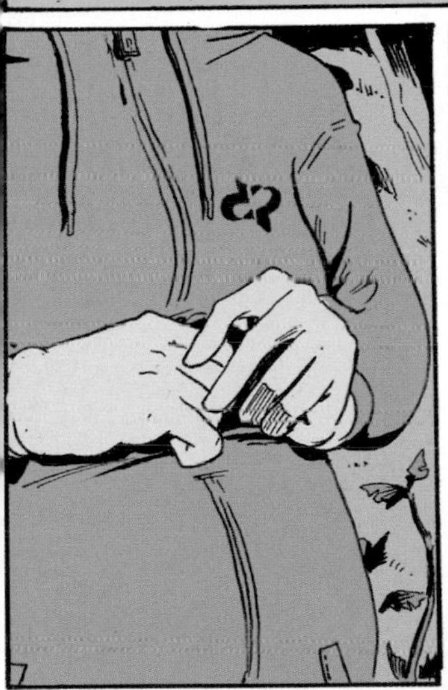

KRR

Carmen can be very charming. I know.
But she changes her story to appeal to who she's talking to.
When I met her it was all about being carefree and not being restrained by responsiblities of the adult world.

I'm sure she told you-
How do I know you're not the one who changes his story?

You talk about not trusting what Carmen says because I just met her and everything,

But you're doing the same thing with this rando.

You're a hypocrite.
Andrea...

I'm finding that fairy ring with or without you.

Let her go.

Then you can be rid of me, Liam.

That's what you wanted, right?

Darra! Get out of here!

Darra, you're Andrea's friend.

You're... you're floating.

Darra! You have to leave! Now!

THUMM!
CRASH
SNAP

Hi.

Darra...

Stop it!

HA HA HA HA!

WHAT THE HELL IS GOING ON?!

I'm just giving Liam what I promised.

What... what just happened?

Ohgodoh godohgod ohgod

Are you okay?
I think so. I'm really tired though.

We-we have to find Carmen's fairy circle. We need to do it now! Oh god!

I'm taking her home so she can rest.

That won't work.

She won't get better unless we stop Carmen!

Then why didn't you stop her when she showed up!

Because her fairy circle is the only way! We have to find it!

Says you! But how do we know that's true!?

Haven't you been paying attention?!

Carmen is playing you! Like she played me!

I'm trying to stop her.

I'm taking her home.

We have 24 hours to stop Carmen.

Or she won't get better.

How are you feeling?
Okay, I think.

I... I'm sorry for calling you a hypocrite earlier.

And um... I guess you were right about Carmen.

So I'm sorry she did whatever it is she did to you.

And I'm not trying to leave you behind.

Well?

Aren't you going to say something?!

Yes.

And?

Can't I take a night off?
From what?

Darra?

A night off from what?

Okay. I'm gonna eat dinner outside.

DARRA!

Ah! What?!

Are you okay?
I just told you I was.
438

I do feel kinda woozy but I'm fine.

I'll be fine after I get some rest.

BU

RIP
206 NHS

CINEMA

Padre
Orgull

Mujer Divina

2nd
Award
for Excellence
in Science CAMP.

CRK
CRK
Who's there?
It's me, Andrea.
What do you want?
There's something wrong with Darra. Seriously wrong.
While walking home there was a moment where she wasn't responding to me and was talking nonsense.
What did Carmen do to her?

Come on.
Carmen is stopping me from getting older and has been for 100 years.
What's that have to do with Darra?
Because Carmen needs to get time from some where so I can have more.
What?

She takes time from other people and gives it to me.
So she takes a day or two away and the victim is left out of sync with the rest of the world.
There's a guy, Steve, and he talks to people who aren't there. But they are ACTUAL people, not like made up people.
They're like our neighbors, they just aren't there when he is talking to them.
How could you do that to other people?
Is that what is gonna happen to Darra?
Y-yes.

I DIDN'T KNOW!
I was a scared kid and I didn't know what Carmen would do.
She just told me I could get what I wanted but didn't tell me how.
A lot of people had their lives ruined because I was a stupid kid.
That's why I have to stop her.

Do you know where to look?
Kinda. A lot of the landmarks have changed though.
Carmen had the same problem. At least we both know it's near the old hospital.
And Beaver Brook.
What?
I fell in the brook while walking home. My mom yelled at me for getting soaked when it was cold out.

Okay. We're in the wrong place.
I distinctly remember it being in the woods next to the hospital.
BUT they built a bunch of houses in the middle of the woods since then.
Cedar Hill Reservation
60
Some sort of Club
Mill st
Belmont
Beaver brook
Reservation
Waverly
So these woods don't have Beaver Brook in them. The woods on the other side of your map do.
Oh.
How far did you walk from the brook to the road?
Um... I don't remember it being long.
It's probably not far off the walking trail. We should meet up tomorrow morning. Where the brook is close to the walking trail.

I'm going to keep looking for the spot but I need a few things.
I need candles the right size and color and salt. A lot of it.
Should be easy enough to get.

Liam...
uh...
Good
luck.
Thanks.

Liam!

Did you find it?
Yes. Did you bring everything?

Yup. Candles and salt.

We got a fire extinguisher too.

In case one of the candles falls over.

How are you feeling?
Um, fine.

Why does everyone keep asking me that today?

I already told you-
Carmen did something to me. But I honestly don't notice anything different.

Come on. The fairy circle is this way.

Nothing special. I'm just hanging out with Andrea today.

We're trying to find crayfish in the woods for science class.

Hey, Darra!

We'll be car-Huh?

What?
It's nothing. Let's keep going.

Here.

We need to put and light candles at North, then East, then West.

Then we need to put salt on the fairy circle to both bind Carmen and stop the fairy circle from growing back. Then we light a candle at the south end.

North is that way.

So this is East, right?
Yeah.

I think the salt has to start at North and go counter-clockwise.

Done.

Oh good.

You found it!

I knew
you wo-

Oh.

Liam...

What do
we do now?

Yeah, Liam. What DO you DO now?

We keep her here. Trapped.

For how long?

Until sunset. If she is trapped she can't fullfill her end of our deal.

But then it will be too late for Darra!
Liam, did you lie to these poor girls?

No, Darra has until midnight.

I have until midnight to what?

Yesterday, you said 24 hours.

Which is it Liam?

Hmmmmm?
I...

All the stories say spells firm up or fall apart by midnight.

All the stories? What stories?

How do we know they're true?

I don't know.

HAHAHAHAHA
HAHAHAH

But it's the only way I've heard to stop her. And if we don't stop her she'll just keep hurting other people.

Even if it's too late for Darra?!

Yes.

Liam's right. If what Carmen did to me is that bad,

then even if we can't undo it,

we should try to stop it from happening to other people.

So let's wait until sunset.

Uh... where's Carmen?

She's up there.

What's she doing?
I don't know.

Crap!
THE

THE TOM LYLE BAND

Darra, give me the fire extinguisher!

We probably shouldn't be here.

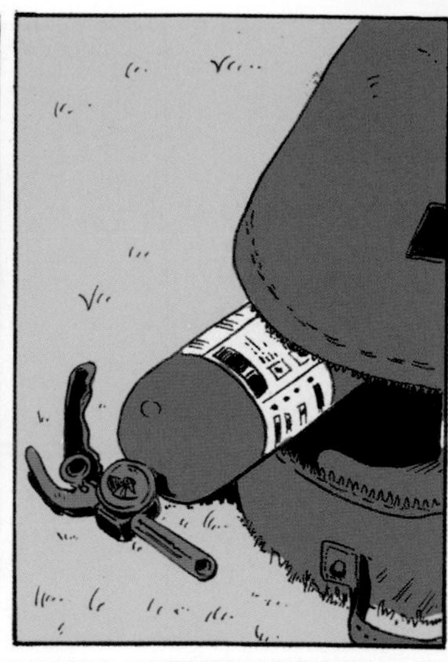

She's going to be stuck like that.

Unless...

You wanted me to fix her.

This um, is Liam.
FFFOOMMMMSSHH

The one who knows Carmen.

Liam, ... do you like LIVE here?
FSH
FOOSH
FOMMSH

I can help both of you get out of here.

This is my friend Andrea.

Don't you want to save your friend.
We were looking for that fairy circle you told me about.

Don't listen to her.

She's just trying to manipulate you.

And he's just using you to get rid of me.
THE

He doesn't care about your friend.

THE TOM LYLE BAND

I...

Andrea, please listen.

I know you want more than what this town can offer but...

Darra...
THE

No.

But you're so eager to rush ahead that you don't see any of the red flags lining the way.

And you don't realize what you are leaving behind.

Hey...
THE
TOM

Oh god! What happened?
THE
TOM

No!

Andrea! Please!

Tell me what you want.

Anything. Just...

Just tell me...

Please...

Let me stay.

THE
TOM

I don't want to go back.

I really can give you anything...
I...

THE TOM LYLE BAND

How do we know she's gone?
I donno.
THE TOM

Liam, any ideas?

Um, no.

I'm suddenly really tired though.

THE TOM

Oh... I guess she is gone.

What should we do?
I haven't the slightest idea.
THE TOM

Don't worry about me.

Just time catching up with me, I suppose.

We can't just leave him here.

Are you okay?
THE TOM

I feel a little bad.
STARS
STARS

For both of them.

But you're okay? You don't feel woozy or anything?
No.

Okay.

Hello! My friend and I are at Beaver Brook reserve, a little off the trail.

I found an old man next to a tree.

He's not moving.

Okay, we'll meet you at the East Entrance.

Paramedics are coming. We got to meet them.
THE TOM
Okay.
Yes, I'm still here.
the

About the Artists

Kel McDonald *(writer)* has been working in comics for over a decade—most of that time has been spent on their webcomic *Sorcery 101*. More recently, they have organized the *Cautionary Fables and Fairytales* anthology series (also available from Iron Circus), while writing and drawing. They have worked on the comic *Buffy: The High School Years*. They recently finished creator-owned series *Misfits of Avalon* for Dark Horse Comics. They're currently working on their self-published series *The City Between*. You can find their work at kelmcdonald.com.

Jose Pimienta *(artist)* Jose Pimienta resides in Glendale, California where they draw comics, storyboards and sketches for visual development. They have worked with Random House Graphic, Iron Circus Comics, Dark Horse Comics, Disney Digital Network, and more. www.josepimienta.com

Character Designs

by Jose Pimienta